White Owl and Blue Mouse

Jean Joubert

White Owl
and Blue Mouse

Illustrations by Michel Gay

Translation by Denise Levertov

ZOLAND BOOKS, INC.
Cambridge, Massachusetts

First North American edition published in 1990 by
Zoland Books, Inc.
384 Huron Avenue,
Cambridge, Massachusetts 02138

Originally published in French as Hibou blanc et souris bleue
Copyright © 1978 by L'Ecole des Loisirs
English translation copyright © 1990 by Denise Levertov

Library of Congress Catalog Card Number: 90-70710
ISBN 0-944072-13-5

FIRST EDITION
Printed in the United States of America

Once upon a time there was an old castle built of white stone with slate-roofed turrets. On one side of it was a lake and a forest, on the other a countryside of farms, fields, and windmills.

In an attic room of this castle lived a white owl: a big fat owl with big round eyes, a hooked beak, and two tufts of feathers on top of his head. During the day, owls can't see. Their eyes close. They sleep. They think things over.

So—this owl lived in the attic, which was full of furniture, chests, statues,

and dust. And all day he slept in a closet
where he'd made himself a feather bed.
He slept or thought about things.

But when night fell, his eyes opened
very wide: yellow and black his eyes
were. And he went out to hunt mice.

For he liked mice very much; he had
already eaten more than a thousand.

One evening, the owl woke up, yawned, opened the closet door and slowly crossed the attic. And the little children who lived in the castle were so scared when they heard his footsteps that they hid their heads under the blankets.

He opened the little attic window, stuck his beak out, and saw that it was night.

"White owl, gray owl—mice look out! Now's the time the owl's about!"

The countryside lay silent, the wind caressed the tops of the trees and a great round moon was strolling through the sky.

The owl hopped up onto the window-sill, stretched out his wings and flew out.

"Who, who, who, who—who, who, who."

The mother mouse said to her children, who were running about the field looking for grains of wheat, "Here comes that wicked owl. Quick, get back in our hole!"

"Yes, mama!"

"What a misery it is! In the daytime the cat lies in wait for us, and at night, when the cat's asleep, the owl comes to hunt us. Quick, quick, get back in!"

"Yes, mama!"

And all the mice rushed deep down
into their hole—except for the youngest,
who was a blue mouse and the cleverest
one of the family.

She watched the owl flying in the moonlight, and said to herself that things couldn't go on this way;

this wicked bird who ate all the mice
must be driven away from this part of
the world.

But how?

She heard the owl's "Who, who,
who, who—who, who, who, who."

"I have an idea," she said to herself.

She climbed onto the big white rock
at the edge of the field and waited there,
all blue.

All at once the owl saw her.

"Aha, a mouse. And it seems to be blue! Well, gray or blue, I'm going to eat it."

And swiftly he swooped down, with his beak sticking out in front of him ready to snap up the mouse, but just

at that moment she leapt to one side
and bam! the owl's head banged into
the rock.

"Ay ay ay!" cried the owl, who had a
big bump on his forehead.

"Hee hee hee!" laughed the mouse.

By this time she was some distance
away, under a tree; she looked at the
owl out of her little eyes.

"You fresh mouse, that's enough out
of you! Come here and be eaten!"

"Come and get me," said the mouse.

The owl rushed towards her, but he hadn't noticed a branch, which whipped across his beak.

"Ouch ouch ouch!" cried the owl.

"Hee hee hee," laughed the mouse.

She ran still farther away, and the owl
went after her. This time, he almost
caught her just as they got to the edge
of the pond, but she disappeared into a
hole and the owl fell into the water,
right in the middle of a crowd of frogs.

Ploof! He was up to
his eyes in water.
"Hee hee hee!"
laughed the mouse.

The owl was furious; and, besides, he was hungry. The mouse ran quickly, quickly across a meadow and the owl ran quickly, quickly after her; under a hedge, into the bushes she ran, faster

and faster. And when he couldn't see
her at all, he heard "hee hee hee" from
somewhere behind him—and off they
started again, faster than ever.

And so the chase went on, all through
the night. By now they were far from
the castle and, lo and behold, it was
almost daylight. The hills turned pink.
A red sun rose in the sky.

The owl couldn't see clearly anymore.
His eyes closed. He was lost. He
couldn't find the way back to his attic.

Far off he heard the mouse laughing:

"Owl white,
Owl gray,
Wicked owl,
You're lost today!
Hee hee hee!"

Then the owl took flight heavily and went to perch in a tree in the middle of a field, to hide among the leaves and wait for the next night.

But it was a dead tree; it didn't have any leaves. One could see the white owl from miles away across the flat land.

A pedlar came along the road with his horse and cart. He saw the owl. "An owl," he said to himself, "what luck! I'll catch it and sell it."

He took a stick and a sack, went up

to the tree and poked the owl off his
branch into the sack. Ploof! Like that.
  Now the owl was a prisoner.

The pedlar drove on towards the town,
clippety clop. In the town square
there was a circus.

30

"I've a nice owl to sell," the pedlar said to the ringmaster. "For ten dollars it's yours."

"Let's take a look," said the ringmaster.

So the pedlar opened the sack. The owl's eyes hurt him. He waved his wings weakly. He couldn't understand at all what was happening to him. He was afraid.

"I'll give you six," said the ringmaster.

"Six?" said the pedlar. "Six dollars for a white owl! You'll have to give me at least eight dollars."

"Six dollars is six dollars."

"And a white owl's a white owl!"

"Well, all right, I'll give you seven," said the ringmaster.

"Done," said the pedlar.

And the ringmaster put the owl in his
menagerie, in a little cage made of gold
wire, and cried, "Come and see, come
and see, children! A nickel to see the
white owl!"

The children of the town went in to
see the owl, who still couldn't figure out
what was happening. They talked and
laughed and made rude faces at him.
  "Have you seen the white owl?"
  "How ugly he is!"
  "How big he is!"
  But the owl thought
about his attic
and was very sad.

The little mouse had gone home.
She told the whole story to her mother
and sisters. And that morning the mice
held a big party in their house, and sang

and danced because they knew the
wicked owl would not come back
and eat them.

The circus travelled from town to
town: three green vans pulled by horses,
followed by the camel, the elephant, and
the giraffe.

And in the first van, in his gold-wire
cage, was the owl. He was sad, that
owl. He would have liked to escape, but
the cage was shut tight.

38

He thought
about his attic:
his feather bed in
the closet, the
little window he
used to open each
evening. And he
thought of the
round moon
in the night sky.

"Cruel mouse,
wicked mouse,"
he said to him-
self, "what a
trick you played
on me. Now I'm
in a cage, and
how bored I am!"

40

Then he shut his
eyes and went
back to sleep.

At night, the
circus tent was
set up in the
main square of
the town they'd
come to.

Music played,
and children
came to the
menagerie to see
the sad white
owl.

Meanwhile, the blue mouse went walking in the meadows by night. But it was strange—she too felt sad,

the little mouse. No more owl in the
sky to go "Who, who, who." She too
was bored.

One evening, she was *so* bored that
she took off all by herself across the
countryside. She arrived at a little town,
and there in the main square was a circus.

"A circus! What fun! I'll go and see the menagerie."

And *frrt,* she slipped into the van. There were cages everywhere. In the first one was a turtle, in the second a fox, in the third a monkey, in the fourth an owl. A white owl.

"My owl!"

"Who, who, who," said the owl sadly. And he looked so unhappy that the blue mouse started to cry.

"How thin he is! And almost gray! Oh, it's my fault!"

"Do you want to help me?" asked the owl.

"Yes, yes. What can I do for you?"

"Open the door of my cage."

"Impossible—it's locked."

"Then gnaw the bars!"

"Impossible—they're made of wire."

"Then what's to be done?"

"What's to be done?"

"Listen," said the owl, "I'm longing
for my attic. You could go and take
a look at my attic in the castle, take a
good look at everything, and come back
and tell me about it."

"I'll go right away. I'll be back by
sunrise."

"By sunrise? Go quickly! I'll be
waiting. Watch out for
the cat."

$\mathbf{A}$nd the blue mouse ran fast, fast, along the road, between the trees, and under the bushes, through the forest and

the fields, quick, quick, quick toward
the castle whose slate-roofed turrets she
could see shining in the moonlight.

She climbed up to the attic. She
scurried across the floor and looked all
round her: the feather bed in the closet,
the statues, the chests, the books, the
dust, the little closed window and,
through the glass, a full moon round as
an owl's eye.

When she got back to the circus the
day was breaking. There were heavy
black clouds in the sky and streaks of
lightning. And the blue mouse ran fast,
fast, fast, and managed to arrive just
before the rain.

She scurried into the van.
"Is it you?" said the owl.
"It's me!" said the mouse.
"What did you see in the attic?"
"Everything."
"Tell me."
"I saw statues."
"And what else?"
"I saw books."
"Come closer. I'm a bit deaf.
What else?"

The blue mouse clambered into the cage. "I saw chests, and furniture, and dust, and a closet with a little feather bed in it."

54

"That's right," said the owl. "But
come a bit closer. I can hardly hear in
this storm. Climb onto my shoulder,
right by my ear."

And the mouse climbed onto his
shoulder.

"I saw a little window," said the
mouse, "and the moon, round as an
eye, like the eye of—of an owl." And
just then the owl swivelled his head
around, opened his big beak and . . .

"Here comes the rain," he said. "Thank you, blue mouse. I shall never forget what you've done for me. Listen carefully. I'm going to make you a promise. You know how much I like to eat mice—"

The blue mouse had forgotten! All at once she was scared and began to tremble.

"You're shivering. Are you cold?" said the owl.

"Yes . . . yes, I'm cold," said the mouse.

"Snuggle in among my feathers."

She snuggled in among his feathers, and it was soft and warm; but she still trembled.

"I was just about to make you a promise," said the owl. "I promise never to eat mice again."

How happy the mouse was to hear
that!

"Well," she said, "then I'm going to
stay with you always. At night I'll sleep
on your shoulder, and in the daytime I'll
go and explore the circus and the town,
and I'll tell you all I see."

"How nice you are, blue mouse," said
the owl.

The days went by. The mouse told the owl how she'd seen the elephant scratching his back, the giraffe eating an apple, the camel rolling in the dust, the children playing hopscotch, the ring-master seeing how far he could spit. And the owl was glad to hear all that.

But he often said, "I can't help it; I'm
always thinking about my attic."
"But what's to be done?"
"That's right: there's nothing we can
do about it . . ."

However, one night the mouse noticed that the ringmaster had forgotten to turn the key of the owl's cage. She climbed onto the lock, and leant against the cage with all her strength.

The door opened.

"Owl, owl," she cried, "the door is open."

"Open?"

"Yes . . . But now you'll go away and I'll be left alone!"

"Come with me! Climb on my back and hold onto my feathers."

The blue mouse gripped the owl's feathers as tight as she was able. The owl came out of his cage, crossed the van, and went down the steps of the van into the square.

The air was soft, the night was clear.
Not a sound in the village.

Then the owl opened his wings wide
and, carrying his friend the blue mouse
with him, flew up towards the moon
and the stars.